Our Little Korean Cousin

H. Lee M. Pike

OUR LITTLE KOREAN COUSIN

CHAPTER I.

SOME QUEER THINGS

Yung Pak was the very queer name of a queer little boy who lived in a queer house in a queer city. This boy was peculiar in his looks, his talk was in a strange tongue, his clothes were odd in colour and fit, his shoes were unlike ours, and everything about him would seem to you very unusual in appearance. But the most wonderful thing of all was that he did not think he was a bit queer, and if he should see one of you in your home, or at school, or at play, he would open wide his slant eyes with wonder at your peculiar ways and dress. The name of the country in which this little boy lived is Korea.

One thing about Yung Pak, though, was just like little boys everywhere. When he first came to his home in the Korean city, a little bit of a baby, his father and mother were very, very glad to see him. Your father and mother gave you no warmer welcome than the parents of this little Korean baby gave to him.

Perhaps Yung Pak's father did not say much, but any one could have seen by his face that he was tremendously pleased. He was a very dignified man, and his manner was nearly always calm, no matter how stirred up he might have felt in his mind. This was one of the rare occasions when his face expanded into a smile, and he immediately made a generous offering of rice to the household tablets.

All Koreans pay great honour to their dead parents, and tablets to their memory are placed in some room set apart for the purpose. Before these tablets sacrifices are offered. Yung Pak's father would have been almost overwhelmed with terror at thought of having no one to worship his memory and present offerings before his tablet.

It is to be feared that if, instead of Yung Pak, a little daughter had come to this Korean house, the father and the mother would not have been so pleased. For, strange as it may seem to you who live in homes where little daughters and little sisters are petted and loved above all the rest of the family, in Korea little girls do not receive a warm welcome, though the mothers will cherish and fondle them—as much from pity as from love. The mothers know better than any one else how hard a way the little girl will have to travel through life.

But it is Yung Pak we want to tell you about.

As his father was a wealthy man, all the comforts and luxuries which could be given to a Korean baby were showered on this tiny boy.

One of the queer things, though, was that he had no little cradle in which he might be rocked to sleep. And you know that all babies, especially little babies, sleep a great deal. So how do you suppose Yung Pak's mother used to put him to sleep in this land where cradles were unknown? She put him on the bed and patted him lightly on the stomach. This she called to-tak, to-tak.

As Yung Pak grew older he was given many toys, among them rattles, drums, flags, and dolls, just as you had them. Some of the toys, though, were very peculiar ones—different from anything you ever saw. He had little tasselled umbrellas, just like the big one his father used when he walked out in the sun. He also had little fringed hats and toy chariots with fancy wheels. One of Yung Pak's favourite toys was a wooden jumping-jack with a pasteboard tongue. By pulling a string the tongue was drawn in and a trumpet carried up to the mouth.

Another favourite toy was a tiger on wheels. Tiger-hunting, by the way, was considered great sport by Yung Pak's father. It was a very dangerous one, too, and sometimes lives were sacrificed in his efforts to capture or to kill this fierce wild beast. Sometimes the animal was caught in a trap which was nothing less than a hut of logs with a single entrance. In the roof of the hut heavy beams would be placed on a forked stick. The bait—a young lamb or kid—would be tied beneath the beams. The moment the bait was touched, down would come the heavy timber—smash—on the tiger's head.

But Yung Pak's tiger was ferocious only in looks. It was made of paper pulp and painted with bright stripes. This harmless image of a fierce beast Yung Pak would pull about the floor with a string by the hour.

All his pets were not of wood and paper. Real live animals he had. Puppies and kittens, of course. His greatest pet, though, was a monkey. What little boy ever saw a monkey that he didn't want for his own? So when Yung Pak's father made him a present of a monkey—a real monkey—alive—he just danced with glee.

This monkey was not a very large one,—not over a foot high,—but he could cut capers and play tricks equal to any monkey you ever saw travelling with an organ-grinder. He was dressed in a scarlet jacket, and he was always with Yung Pak, except sometimes when he would try to plague him by breaking away and running—perhaps to the house-top or to the neighbour's garden.

After a little while Yung Pak got used to these "monkey shines," and he knew that his pet would not stay away long after mealtime.

As Yung Pak grew older he was allowed to play with other boys of his own age. A favourite sport was Hunting the Ring. In this game the boys would get together quite a large heap of sand. In this sand one of them would hide a ring, and then the urchins would all get slender sticks and poke around in the pile trying to find the ring. Whoever succeeded in getting the ring on his stick won the game, and carried the prize home as a sign of victory.

Sometimes Yung Pak would be the winner, and then he would march home with great glee and show the trophy to his father.

One of the first things Yung Pak was taught was to be respectful to his father. Never was he allowed to fail in this duty in the least. This does not seem strange when we know what a sober, serious, dignified man Yung Pak's father was. It would not do to allow his son to do anything that would upset his dignity, though he loved him very much indeed.

It was far different with the boy's mother. Her little boy soon learned that her wishes counted for very little in the family, and she never ventured to rebuke him, no matter how seriously he might offend her or what naughty thing he might do.

One queer thing about Yung Pak was the way he used to wear his hair. While still very young his head was shaved, except a little round spot on the very crown. Here it was allowed to grow, and as years went by it grew quite long, and was braided in two plaits down his back.

When Yung Pak grew to be a man the long hair was knotted up on top of his head, and for this reason many people call Koreans "Top-knots." But of this arrangement of the hair we shall tell more farther on.

CHAPTER II.

YUNG PAK'S HOME

Ki Pak, Yung Pak's father, was one of the king's officials. On this account his home was near the great palace of the king, in the city of Seoul, the capital of the country.

This city did not look much like the ones in which you live. There were no wide streets, no high buildings, no street-cars. Instead, there were narrow, dirty lanes and open gutters. Shopkeepers not only occupied both sides of the crowded streets, but half their wares were exposed in and over the dirty gutters. Grain merchants and vegetable dealers jostled each other in the streets themselves. In and about among them played the boys of the city, not even half-clothed in most cases. There were no parks and playgrounds for them such as you have. Often, too, boys would be seen cantering through the streets, seated sidewise on the bare backs of ponies, caring nothing for passers-by, ponies, or each other—laughing, chatting, eating chestnuts. Other boys would be carrying on their heads small round tables covered with dishes of rice, pork, cabbage, wine, and other things.

A STREET IN SEOUL

Around the city was a great wall of stone fourteen miles in length. In some places it clung to the edges of the mountains, and then dropped into a deep ravine, again to climb a still higher mountain, perhaps. In one direction it enclosed a forest, in another a barren plain. Great blocks were the stones, that had been in place many, many years. It must have taken hundreds and thousands of men to put them in position, and, though the wall was hundreds of years old, it was still well preserved. It was from twenty-five to forty feet high. The wall was hung from one end of the city to the other with ivy, which looked as if it had been growing in its place centuries before Yung Pak was born.

In the wall were eight gates, and at each one a keeper was stationed at all hours of the day and night. No persons could come in or go out unless their business was known to those who had charge of the passage.

Every evening, at sunset, the gates were closed, and during the night no one was allowed to pass through in either direction.

A curious ceremony attended the closing of these gates. They were never shut till the king had been notified that all was well on the north, on the south, on the east, and on the west. As there were no telegraph lines, another way had to be provided by which messages might be quickly sent. Bonfires upon the surrounding hills were used as signals. By these fires the king was told if all were well in his kingdom, and every evening, as soon as the sun was set, four beacon-fires on a hill within the walls told the news as it was flashed to them from the mountains outside. Then four officers, whose business it was to report to the king the message of the fires, hastened to him, and with great ceremony and much humility announced that all was well. On this the royal band of music would strike up its liveliest airs, and a great bell would toll its evening warning. This bell was the third largest in the world, and for five centuries it had given the signal for opening and closing the gates of Seoul, the chief city of the "Land of the Morning Radiance."

At the stroke of the bell, with a great clang the gates were shut, and strong bars were placed across the inner sides, not to be removed until at early dawn the bell again gave its signal to the keepers.

To little Yung Pak, the loud tones of the bell meant more even than to the sentinels at the gates. He knew that not only was it a signal for the closing of the city gates, but it was also a warning that bedtime was at hand.

The house in which Yung Pak lived was a very fine one, although the grounds were not as spacious as those of many houses in the outskirts of the city. But its walls were of stone, whereas many of the houses of Seoul had walls of paper.

Yes, actually walls of paper!

But this paper was a very tough, fibrous substance, and would resist quite a heavy blow as well as keep out the cold. Its slight cost brought it within the means of the poorer people.

In some parts of Korea the houses were built of stout timbers, the chinks covered with woven cane and plastered with mud. Neat hedges of interlaced boughs surrounded them. The chimney was often simply a hollow tree, not attached to the house.

Ki Pak's house was not only built of stone, but about it were four walls of stone, about five feet high, to help keep out intruders. The wall was surmounted by a rampart of plaited bamboo. In this wall were three gates, corresponding to entrances into the house itself. One gate, the largest, on the north side, was used only by Ki Pak himself, though after he grew older Yung Pak could enter this gate with his father. The second gate, on the east, was used by the family and friends of Ki Pak. The third and smallest gate was reserved for the use of the servants.

The roof of this house was not covered with shingles, but with clay tiles, coloured red. Many houses in the city had simply a roof-covering of thatched straw.

The house was but a single story high, but in this respect the king's palace itself was no better. There were three divisions to the house. One was for the use of the men, a second for the women of the family, and a third for the servants. Each division had a suitable number of rooms for its occupants.

Yung Pak's own sleeping-room was a dainty affair, with its paper walls, tiger-skin rugs upon the stone floor, and the softest of mats and silk and wadded cotton coverings for his couch.

This couch, by the way, was another queer affair. It was built of brick! Beneath it were pipes or flues connected with other pipes which ran beneath the whole house. Through these flues were forced currents of hot air from a blaze in a large fireplace at one end of the house. The chimney was at the other end, and thus a draught of hot air constantly passed beneath the floors in cold weather. On warm nights Yung Pak would pile his mats upon the floor and sleep as comfortably as ever you did on the softest feather bed your grandmother could make.

The windows of Ki Pak's house were not made of glass, but were small square frames covered with oiled paper. These frames fitted into grooves so that they could be slid back and forth, and in warm weather the windows were always left open. The doors were made of wood, though in many houses paper or plaited bamboo was used.

When Yung Pak ate his meals, he sat upon a rug on the floor with his father and such male guests as might be in the house. The women never ate with them. Their meals were served in their own rooms.

A servant would bring to each person a sang, or small low table. Instead of a cloth, on each table was a sheet of fine glazed paper which had the appearance of oiled silk. This paper was made from the bark of the mulberry-tree. It was soft and pliable, and of such a texture that it could be washed easier than anything else, either paper or cloth. On this were placed dishes of porcelain and earthen ware. There were no knives or forks, but in their place were chop-sticks such as the Chinese used. Spoons also were on the table. A tall and long-spouted teapot was always the finest piece of ware.

On the dining-tables of the poorer people of Korea the teapot was never seen, for, strange as it may seem, in this land situated between the two greatest tea-producing countries of the world, tea is not in common use.

All Koreans have splendid appetites, and probably if you should see Yung Pak eating his dinner you would criticize his table manners. He not only ate a large amount of food, but ate it very rapidly — almost as if he feared that some one might steal his dinner before he could dispose of it. And you would think that he never expected to get another square meal!

But it was not Yung Pak's fault that he was such a little glutton. In his youngest days, when his mother used to regulate his food, she would stuff him full of rice. Then she would turn him over on his back and paddle his stomach with a ladle to make sure that he was well filled!

CHAPTER III.

A GLIMPSE OF THE KING

Yung Pak's earliest days were spent very much as are those of most babies, whether they live in Korea or America. Eating and sleeping were his chief occupations.

When he grew old enough to run about, his father employed for him a servant, Kim Yong, whose business it was to see that no harm came to the child. For several years the two were constantly together, even sleeping in the same room at night.

Once when Yung Pak and his attendant were out for their daily walk their attention was attracted by the sound of music in the distance.

"What is that music?" asked Yung Pak.

"That is the king's band. It must be that there is going to be a procession," was Kim Yong's reply.

"Oh, I know what it is," said Yung Pak. "The king is going to the new Temple of Ancestors. My father said the tablets on which the king's forefathers' names are engraved are to be put in place to-day."

"Let us hurry so as to get into a place where we can have a good view of the procession."

"Yes, we will; for father told me that this is to be an extra fine one, and he is to be in it himself. I want to see him when he goes by."

By this time Yung Pak and Kim Yong were running as fast as their flowing garments and their dignity would allow them. And everybody else, from the dirtiest street boy to the gravest old man, was hurrying toward the palace gate through which the procession was to come. Yung Pak and Kim Yong were fortunate enough to get a position where they could see the palace gate, and the procession would have to pass by them on its way to the temple.

Meanwhile the band inside the palace walls kept up its music, and the people outside could also hear the shouts of officers giving their orders to guards and soldiers.

Soon there was an extra flourish of the music, and the gate, toward which all eyes had been strained, was suddenly flung wide open with a great clang.

Hundreds of soldiers already lined the streets to keep the crowd back out of the way of the procession.

First through the gate came a company of Korean foot-soldiers, in blue uniforms. Directly after them came a lot of palace attendants in curious hats and long robes of all colours of the rainbow. Some were dressed in blue, some in red, some in orange, some in yellow, some in a mixture of colours. All carried staves bound with streamers of ribbons.

Following the attendants came a line of bannermen, with red flags, on which were various inscriptions in blue; then came drummers and pipe-players dressed in yellow costumes, their instruments decked with ribbons.

Yung Pak next saw more soldiers, dressed in the queerest of ancient costumes; afterward came men with cymbals and bells, cavalrymen on foot, and more palace attendants. Through the whole line were seen many officials, gaudily adorned with plumes, gold lace, gilt fringe, swords, and coloured decorations of all sorts. Many of the officials had on high-crowned hats decorated with bunches of feathers and crimson tassels. These were fastened by a string of amber beads around the throat. Blue and orange and red were the colours of their robes. Then followed more bannermen, drummers, and servants carrying food, fire, and pipes.

All the time there was a tremendous beating of drums and blowing of horns and ringing of bells. The noise was so great that Kim Yong hardly heard Yung Pak when he shouted:

"Oh, I see papa!"

"Where is he?"

"Don't you see him right behind that little man in yellow who is carrying a big blue flag?"

"Oh, yes," said Kim Yong. "He has on a long green robe, and on his turban are long orange plumes."

"Yes; and on both sides of him, in green gauze coats, are his servants. I wonder if he will notice us as he goes by."

"Indeed he will not. At least, if he does see us, he will give no sign, for this is too solemn and important an occasion for him to relax his dignity."

On state occasions Ki Pak could look as sedate and dignified as the most serious official in all Korea; and that is saying a good deal, for in no country do the officials appear more solemn than in this "Land of the Morning Radiance."

Now along came more soldiers, followed by the great nobles of the kingdom, and finally, amid a most terrific beating of drums, a fearful jangling of bells, and a horrid screaming of pipes, the guard of the king himself appeared.

Suddenly all was silent. Drum-beating, pipe-blowing, and shouting all died away. The sound of hurried footsteps alone was heard. All at once into sight came the imperial chair of state. In this chair was the king, but not yet could Yung Pak get a glimpse of his royal master. Yellow silken panels hid him from the view of the curious crowd, and over the top was a canopy of the same description, ornamented with heavy, rich tassels.

This gorgeous chair was much heavier than those used by officials and ordinary citizens, and it took thirty-two men to carry it quickly and safely past the throng to the entrance of the temple. Only a few minutes were necessary for this journey, for the temple was but a short distance from the palace gate, and both were in plain sight of Yung Pak and Kim Yong.

It was only a fleeting glimpse of the king that they got, as he passed from his chair to the temple gate; but this was enough to repay Yung Pak for the rushing and the crowding and the waiting that he had been obliged to endure. Rare indeed were these glimpses of his Majesty, and they afforded interest and excitement enough to last a long while.

But the procession was not over yet. A chair covered with red silk, borne on the shoulders of sixteen chair-men, passed up to the temple.

"Who is in that chair?" asked Yung Pak of his companion.

"The crown prince," was Kim Yong's reply.

"He attends his royal father in all these ceremonies of state."

Yung Pak drew a long breath, but said nothing. He only thought what a fine thing it must be to be a king's son, and wear such gorgeous clothes, and have so many servants at his call.

And then he had a second thought. He would not want to exchange his splendid father for all the glory and magnificence of the king's court.

After the king and the crown prince, with their attendant officials and servants and priests, had gone into the temple, Yung Pak and Kim Yong did not stay longer at their post. The order of the procession had broken, and the king and his immediate retinue would return privately to the palace after he should pay homage and offer sacrifice to the spirits of his ancestors.

CHAPTER IV.

YUNG PAK AT SCHOOL

Little Korean boys have to go to school, just as you do, though they do not study in just the same way. You would be surprised if you were to step into a Korean schoolroom. All the boys sit upon the floor with their legs curled up beneath them. Instead of the quiet, silent scholars, you would hear a loud and deafening buzz. All the pupils study out loud. They not only do their studying aloud, but they talk very loud, as if each one were trying to make more noise than his neighbour.

The Koreans call this noise kang-siong, and it seems almost deafening to one unused to it. You would think the poor teacher would be driven crazy, but he seems as calm as a daisy in a June breeze.

ALL THE BOYS SIT UPON THE FLOOR

The Korean boys have to have "tests" and examinations just as you do. When a lad has a good lesson, the teacher makes a big red mark on his paper, and he carries it home with the greatest pride,—just as you do when you take home a school paper marked "100."

But Yung Pak was not allowed to share the pleasures and the trials of the boys in the public school.

One day, soon after he was six years old, his father sent for him to come to his private room,—perhaps you would call it a study or library. With Yung Pak's father was a strange gentleman, a young man with a pleasant face and an air of good breeding.

"This," said Ki Pak to his son as he entered the room, "is Wang Ken. I have engaged him to be your teacher, or tutor. The time has come for you to begin to learn to read and to cipher and to study the history and geography of our country."

Yung Pak made a very low bow, for all Korean boys are early taught to be courteous, especially to parents, teachers, and officials.

In this case he was very glad to show respect to his new tutor, for he liked his appearance and felt sure that they would get on famously together.

More than that, though he liked to play as well as any boy, he was not sorry that he was going to begin to learn something. Even at his age he had ambitions, and expected that sometime he would, like his father, serve the king in some office.

Wang Ken was equally well pleased with the looks of the bright boy who was to be his pupil, and told Yung Pak's father that he believed there need be no fear but what they would get on well together, and that the boy would prove a bright scholar.

To Wang Ken and his pupil were assigned a room near Ki Pak's library, where Yung Pak would spend several hours each day trying his best to learn the Korean A B C's.

The first book he had to study was called "The Thousand Character Classic." This was the first book that all Korean boys had to study, and was said to have been written by a very wise man hundreds of years ago. A strange thing about it was that it was composed during one night, and so great was the wise man's struggle that his hair and beard turned white during that night. When Yung Pak was told this fact he was not a bit surprised. He thought it was hard enough to have to learn what was in the book, to say nothing of writing it in the beginning.

At the same time that Yung Pak was learning to read, he was also learning to write. But you would have been amused if you could have seen his efforts. The strangest thing about it was that he did not use a pen, but had a coarse brush on a long handle. Into the ink he would dip this brush and then make broad marks on sheets of coarse paper. You would not be able to understand those marks at all. They looked like the daubs of a sign-painter gone crazy.

Later on, Yung Pak had to study the history and geography of his country. Some of the names he had to learn would amuse you very much. The name of the province of Haan-kiung, for instance, meant Perfect Mirror, or Complete View Province. Kiung-sang was the Korean name for Respectful Congratulation Province, and Chung-chong meant Serene Loyalty Province. One part of Korea, where the inhabitants were always peaceable and unwarlike, was called Peace and Quiet Province, or, in the Korean language, Ping-an.

Under Wang Ken's instruction Yung Pak made rapid progress in his studies, and when the boy's father questioned him from time to time as to what he had learned, he was very much pleased, and commended his son for his close attention to his studies.

"Sometime," Ki Pak said to the boy, "if you continue to make such good progress in your studies, you will be able to hold a high position in the service of the king."

In explanation of this remark, you should understand that no young man was able to enter into the government service of Korea until he could pass a very hard examination in many studies.

Many things besides book-learning did Wang Ken teach his pupil. In all the rules of Korean etiquette he was carefully and persistently drilled.

As you have already been told, Yung Pak had from his earliest days been taught the deepest reverence and honour for his father. This kind of instruction was continued from day to day. He was told that a son must not play in his father's presence, nor assume free or easy posture before him. He must often wait upon his father at meal-times, and prepare his bed for him. If the father is old or sickly, the son sleeps near him by night, and does not leave his presence by day. If for any reason the father is cast into prison, the son makes his home near by in order that he may provide such comforts for his unfortunate parent as the prison officials will allow.

If, by chance, the father should be banished from the country for his misdeeds, the son must accompany him at least to the borders of his native land, and in some instances must go with him into exile.

When the son meets his father in the street, he must drop to his knees and make a profound salute, no matter what the state of the roadway. In all letters which the son writes to his father he uses the most exalted titles and honourable phrases he can imagine.

CHAPTER V.

A LESSON IN HISTORY

As you already know, Yung Pak's father intended that his son, when he grew up, should fill a position in the service of the king. To fit him for this work, it was important that the boy should learn all that he could of his country's history.

On this account Yung Pak's tutor had orders to give to the lad each day, during the hours devoted to study, some account of events in the rise and progress of the Korean nation or of its royal families.

You must know that Korea is a very old country, its history dating back hundreds of years before America was discovered by Christopher Columbus.

Now Wang Ken knew that dry history had very few attractions for his young pupil, or any lively boy for that matter, so as far as possible he avoided the repetition of dates and uninteresting events, and often gave to Yung Pak much useful information in story form.

One day, when the time came for the usual history lesson, Wang Ken said to Yung Pak:

"I think that to-day I will tell you the story of King Taijo."

At this Yung Pak's eyes sparkled, and he was all attention in a moment. He thought one of Wang Ken's stories was a great deal better than puzzling over Korean letters or struggling with long strings of figures. The tutor went on:

"When Taijo was born, many, many years ago, our country was not called Korea, but had been given the name of Cho-sen."

Yung Pak had been told that Cho-sen meant Morning Calm, so he asked Wang Ken how it came about that such a peaceful name had been given to his country.

"Why," said Wang Ken, "the name was given to our land years and years ago by the leader of some Chinese settlers, whose name was Ki Tsze. In his native land there had been much violence and war, so with his friends and followers he moved to the eastward and selected this country for his home. Here he hoped to be free from the attacks of enemies and to be able to live a peaceful life. For this reason he chose a name which well expressed its outward position—toward the rising sun—and his own inward feelings,—Cho-sen, or Morning Calm. This is still the official name of our country.

"But to come back to our story of Taijo. At the time of his birth, the rulers of the country were very unpopular because of their wickedness and oppression of the people. There was much suffering on account of the misrule, and the people longed for a deliverer who should restore prosperity to Cho-sen.

"Such a deliverer appeared in the person of Taijo. It is said that even as a boy he surpassed his fellows in goodness, intelligence, and skill in all sorts of boyish games."

Wang Ken improved this opportunity to tell Yung Pak how important it was that all boys should follow such an example.

But while Yung Pak listened with apparent patience, he could hardly conceal his inward desire that the tutor would go on with his story. Like most boys, of all races, he felt that he could get along without the moralizing.

"Hunting with the falcon was one of Taijo's favourite sports. One day, while in the woods, his bird flew so far ahead that its young master lost sight of it. Hurrying on to find it, Taijo discovered a hut beside the path, into which he saw the falcon fly.

"Entering the hut, the youth found a white-bearded hermit priest, who lived here alone and unknown to the outside world. For a moment Taijo was speechless with surprise in the presence of the wise old hermit.

"Seeing his embarrassment, the old man spoke to him in these words:

"'What benefit is it for a youth of your abilities to be seeking a stray falcon? A throne is a richer prize. Betake yourself at once to the capital.'

"Now Taijo knew how to take a hint as well as any boy, so he immediately left the hut of the hermit, forsaking his falcon, and went to Sunto, then the capital of the kingdom.

"As I have already told you, Taijo was a wise youth. He did not rush headlong into the accomplishment of the purpose hinted at by the hermit. Had he done so, and at that time attempted to dethrone the king, he would certainly have been overpowered and slain.

"He took a more deliberate and sensible way. First he enlisted in the army of the king. As he was a young man of courage and strength, he was not long in securing advancement. He rapidly rose through the various grades, until he finally held the chief command of the army as lieutenant-general.

"Of course Taijo did not reach this high station in a month, nor in a year, but many years went by before he attained such an exalted place. Meanwhile he married and had children. Several of these children were daughters."

Wang Ken did not say right here, what he might have said with truth,— that in Korean families girls are considered of very little consequence. But in this case Taijo's daughter proved to be of much help in making her father the king of Cho-sen.

"One of these daughters was married to the reigning king. Thus Taijo became father-in-law to his sovereign. You can easily see that in this relationship he must have had a large influence both over the king and over the people.

"Being a brave man and courageous fighter, Taijo was idolized by his soldiers. He was also very popular with all the people because he was always strictly honest and just in all his dealings with them.

"Taijo proved his bravery and his reliance on the soldiers and on the people by attempting to bring about a change in the conduct of the king, who abused his power and treated his subjects without mercy.

"The king, however, refused to listen to the advice of his father-in-law, and, as a consequence, the hatred of the people for him grew in volume and force every day.

"Meanwhile, the king was having other troubles. In former years, Korea had paid an annual tribute or tax to China, but for some time it had been held back by this king. Consequently the Chinese (or Ming) emperor sent a large army to enforce his demand for the amount of money due him.

"The Korean ruler neglected the matter and finally refused to pay. He then ordered that more soldiers be added to his army, that the Chinese forces might be resisted; but with all his efforts the enemy's army was much the larger. Nevertheless, he ordered Taijo, at the head of his forces, to attack the Chinese. Upon this, Taijo thus addressed his soldiers:

"'Although the order from the king must be obeyed, yet the attack upon the Ming soldiers, with so small an army as ours, is like casting an egg against a rock, and no one of us will return alive. I do not tell you this from any fear of death, but our king is too haughty. He does not heed our advice. He has ordered out the army suddenly without cause, paying no attention to the suffering which wives and children of the soldiers must undergo. This is a thing I cannot bear. Let us go back to the capital, and the responsibility shall fall on my shoulders alone.'

"The soldiers were quite willing to take the advice of their courageous leader, and resolved to obey his orders rather than the king's. They went to the capital, forcibly removed the king from his throne, and banished him to the island of Kang-wa.

"Not yet, however, was Taijo made king. The deposed ruler plotted and planned all kinds of schemes whereby he might be restored to his old position of authority. Taijo heard of some of his plots, and finally did that which would for ever extinguish the authority of the old king or any of his family. He removed from the temple the tablets on which were inscribed the names of the king's ancestors. More than this, he ordered that no more sacrifices be offered to them.

"The king could have suffered no greater insult than this, for, like all Koreans, he held as sacred the memory of his ancestors, and even to speak ill of one of them was an unpardonable crime. But this time he was powerless to resent the indignity or to punish the offender, and consequently he lost what little influence he had been able to retain.

"Taijo was now formally proclaimed king. He was able to make peace with the Chinese emperor, and under his rule the Koreans enjoyed freedom from war and oppression. His descendants still sit upon the throne of Korea."

CHAPTER VI.

THE MONK'S STORY

One evening, after Yung Pak had finished his supper, he sat talking with his father and Wang Ken.

The early evening hour was often spent in this way. It was a time of day when Ki Pak was generally free from any official duty, and he was glad to devote a little time to his son. He would inquire about the boy's studies as well as about his sports, and Yung Pak would regale his father with many an amusing incident or tell him something he had learned during study hours. Sometimes he would tell of the sights he had seen on the streets of Seoul, while on other occasions he would give account of games with his playmates or of his success in shooting with a bow and arrow.

This latter sport was very common with the men and boys of Korea. It was approved by the king for the national defence in time of war, and often rewards were offered by rich men for winners in contests. Most Korean gentlemen had private archery grounds and targets in the gardens near their houses.

Ki Pak had an arrow-walk and target in his garden, and here it was that Yung Pak used to practise almost daily. He often, too, invited other boys to enjoy the sport with him.

At regular times every year public contests in arrow-shooting were held, and costly prizes were offered to the winners by the king. The prizes were highly valued by those who secured them, and Yung Pak looked forward with eager anticipation to the day when he should be old enough and skilful enough to take part in these contests.

While Yung Pak was listening to the conversation between his father and tutor on this evening, a knock was heard.

On opening the door there was seen standing at the entrance a man rather poorly clad in the white garments worn by nearly all the people of Korea. But upon his head, instead of the ordinary cone-shaped hat worn by the men of the country, was a very peculiar structure. It was made of straw and was about four feet in circumference. Its rim nearly concealed the man's face, which was further hidden by a piece of coarse white linen cloth stretched upon two sticks and made fast just below the eyes.

This method of concealing the face, together with the wearing of the immense hat, was a symbol of mourning. Such a sight was not uncommon in the streets of Seoul, and Yung Pak knew well its meaning.

With great courtesy and hospitality Ki Pak invited the stranger within the house.

"I thank you for your kindness," said the visitor. "I am a stranger in your city, a monk from a monastery in Kong-chiu. Your peculiar law not allowing men upon the street after nightfall compels me to seek shelter."

"To that you are entirely welcome, my friend," said Ki Pak, whose hospitable nature would have granted the monk's request, even if sympathy for sorrow and reverence for religion had not also been motives for his action.

"Let me get the man something to eat," said Yung Pak as the monk seated himself upon a mat.

"Certainly, my son; it is always proper to offer food to a guest who takes refuge under our roof."

Quickly the boy sought his mother in the women's apartments, and very soon returned with a steaming bowl of rice, which he placed before the visitor.

This gift of rice was especially pleasing to the traveller, as no dish is held in higher honour in Korea. It is the chief cereal, and the inhabitants say it originated in Ha-ram, China, nearly five thousand years ago. Yung Pak called it Syang-nong-si, which means Marvellous Agriculture. He had learned from Wang Ken that it was first brought to Korea in 1122 B.C.

To the monk the warm food was very refreshing, and after he had eaten a generous amount he entered into conversation with his hosts.

He told of the monastery where he made his home, and his account of the various religious ceremonies and their origin was very interesting to Yung

Pak, who found that the visitor not only knew a great deal of the history of the country, but was also familiar with its fables and legends.

Like many who live in retirement and dwell in a world apart from their fellows, this monk thought the people of former times were superior to the men of his own day. Especially did he praise the kings of years long gone by.

"Do you think," said Yung Pak, "that the old kings were any better than our own gracious ruler?"

Yung Pak was very jealous of the honour of his king.

"Why, yes," replied the monk. "And to prove my statement let me tell you a story:

"Many years ago there was in Cho-sen a king named Cheng-chong. He was celebrated throughout his kingdom for his goodness. It was a habit with him to disguise himself in ordinary clothing and then to go out and mingle with the common people. In this way he was often able to discover opportunities for doing much good to his subjects.

"One night Cheng-chong disguised himself as a countryman, and, taking a single friend along, started out to make a tour of inspection among his people, that he might learn the details of their lives.

"Coming to a dilapidated-looking house, he suspected that within there might be miserable people to whom he could render assistance. Desiring to see the inside of the house, he punched a peep-hole in the paper door. Looking through this hole, the king perceived an old man weeping, a man in mourning garb singing, and a nun or widow dancing.

"Cheng-chong was unable to imagine the cause of these strange proceedings, so he asked his companion to call the master of the house.

"In answer to the summons, the man in mourning made his appearance. The king, with low and respectful salutation, said:

"'We have never before met.'

"'True,' was the reply, 'but whence are you? How is it that you should come to find me at midnight? To what family do you belong?'

"Cheng-chong answered: 'I am Mr. Ni, living at Tong-ku-an. As I was passing before your house I was attracted by strange sounds. Then through a hole in the door I saw an old man crying, a dancing nun, and a man in mourning singing. Why did the nun dance, the bereaved man sing, and the old man weep? I have called you out on purpose to learn the reason of these things.'

"'For what reason do you pry into other people's business?' was the question in reply. 'This is little concern to you. It is past midnight now, and you had better get home as soon as you can.'

"'No, indeed. I admit that it seems wrong for me to be so curious in regard to your affairs, but this case is so very extraordinary that I hope you will not refuse to tell me about it. You may be sure that I shall not betray your confidence.'

"'Alas! why such persistence in trying to learn about other people's business?'

"'It is very important,' replied the king, 'that I should obtain the information I have asked of you. Further than that I cannot explain at present.'"

Yung Pak wanted to interrupt the storyteller here and say that he did not blame the man for objecting to telling his private business, but he had early been taught that it was highly improper for a Korean boy to break into the conversation of his elders.

The monk continued:

"'As you are so urgent in your desire to know the cause of the strange proceedings you have witnessed, I will try to tell you. Poverty has always been a burden upon my family. In my house there has never been sufficient food for a solid meal, and I have not land enough even for an insect to rest upon. I cannot even provide food for my poor old father. This is the reason why my wife, from time to time, has cut off a portion of her hair and sold it for an amount sufficient to buy a bowl of bean soup, which she has generously given to my father. This evening she cut off and sold the last tress of her hair, and thus she is now bald as a nun.'"

Yung Pak already knew that Korean women who devote their lives to religious service kept their hair closely clipped, so the monk did not need to explain his reference to a bald-headed nun.

"'On this account," said the man to Cheng-chong, 'my father broke out into mourning in these words:

"'"Why have I lived to this age? Why did I not die years ago? Why has this degradation come to my daughter-in-law?" Tears accompanied his words. My wife and I tried to console him, and, besides urging him not to weep, she danced for his amusement. I also danced and sang, and thus we diverted the old man's thoughts and caused him to smile. That is the true reason of our queer behaviour. I trust you will not think it strange, and will now go away and leave us to our sorrow.'

"The king was very much impressed by the man's story, particularly with the evidence of such great devotion to his father, even in the time of poverty and misfortune. So he said: 'This is really the most extraordinary instance of filial love that I ever saw. I think you should present yourself at the examination to-morrow.'

"'What examination?'

"'Why, there is to be an examination before the king of candidates for official position. You know that all officials have to pass an examination before they can receive an appointment. Be sure to be there, and you may be fortunate enough to secure a position which will remove all fear of poverty from your household.'

"Having thus spoken, Cheng-chong bade the man good night and went at once to his palace.

"Very early in the morning he caused proclamation to be made that an examination would be held that day, at a certain hour. Notwithstanding the brief time for preparation, when the hour arrived a large number of men presented themselves at the king's palace as candidates.

"In the crowd was the poor man whom the king, in his disguise, had talked with the night before. Though he understood little of the matter, he felt that his visitor of the previous night must have known perfectly about it.

"When all had assembled, the following was announced as the subject of the examination: 'The song of a man in mourning, the dance of a nun, the tears of an old man.'

"With the exception of the poor man, not a single one of the candidates was able to make a bit of sense out of the subject. He alone knew it perfectly well, because of his own personal sad experience. Consequently he was able to turn in a clear essay upon the subject, which, upon examination, the king found to be free from error.

"Cheng-chong then bestowed the degree of doctor upon the man, and ordered that he be brought into his presence.

"Upon the man's appearance, the king asked: 'Do you know who I am? It is I who last night advised you to be present at this examination. Raise your head and look at me.'

"With fixed gaze the man looked at the king, and recognized his benefactor. He at once bowed himself to the ground in gratitude, and in words of the most humble sort returned his thanks.

"'Go at once,' said Cheng-chong, 'and return to your wife and old father. Make them happy with the good news you have for them.'

"This story of royal generosity has been handed down from generation to generation, and I give it to you," concluded the monk, "as an example of the goodness of our ancient kings and the rich inheritance we have from them. True devotion to parents has never been unrewarded in Korea."

His story concluded, the monk expressed a desire to retire for the night. At Ki Pak's command a servant led him to a sleeping-room. Yung Pak and the other members of the family also retired, and were soon buried in peaceful slumber.

CHAPTER VII.

A JOURNEY

It sometimes happened that Ki Pak, in performing his official duties, was obliged to make long journeys to various parts of Korea. One of Yung Pak's greatest pleasures was to listen to the stories which his father used to tell him about these journeys.

When Ki Pak made one of these trips through the country he could not ride on the cars as you do, for there were no railways, with puffing engines and comfortable coaches; neither could he take a carriage drawn by swift and strong horses, for they too were unknown by the Koreans. Even if he had possessed horses and carriage, there were few roads over which they could have been driven. Most of the highways were simply rough paths, over which men usually travelled on foot or on the backs of ponies up and down the hills of the country. It was generally necessary to cross rivers by fording, though, where the water was too deep for this, rude and clumsy ferry-boats were provided. Occasionally, over a narrow stream, a frail footbridge would be built.

You can easily imagine Yung Pak's joy and surprise one day when his father told him that he proposed to take his little son on his next journey.

Ki Pak had been ordered by the king to go to Chang-an-sa, a city among the Diamond Mountains, near the eastern coast of Korea, and about eighty miles from Seoul. In this place was a famous monastery, or temple, which would be an object of much interest and wonder to Yung Pak.

It was decided, also, that Wang Ken should be one of the party. He would be able to explain to Yung Pak many things they might see on the way.

There was much to do to get ready for the journey. It would take four days to cover the distance, and, as hotels were unknown along the route, it was necessary to take along a good supply of provisions, bedding, cooking utensils, and all sorts of things they might need while absent from home.

In addition to getting together all this material, ponies and drivers had to be engaged. Sometimes, when Ki Pak went on short journeys, he was carried in a chair by strong men, who by much practice had become able to endure the fatigue of travel, and of bearing heavy burdens. This chair was very different from the kind you have in your houses. Even a comfortable rocker would not be very nice in which to take a long journey.

The Korean traveller's chair consists of a boxlike frame, of such height that one may sit within in Turkish fashion upon the floor. The roof is of bamboo, covered with painted and oiled paper. The sides also are covered with oiled paper or muslin. In some cases a small stained glass window is set in the side or front, but only rich men can afford this luxury. The curtain in front can be raised or lowered. This serves the double purpose of shutting out the glances of the curious and keeping out the cold air. When the owner can afford it, an ample supply of cushions and shawls makes the clumsy vehicle more comfortable for its occupant.

The chair rests upon two long poles, which hang by straps upon the shoulders of four stout men. Under ordinary circumstances these men can travel with their burden from twenty to thirty miles a day.

Sometimes, also, when Yung Pak's father went about the streets of Seoul, he rode in a chair very similar to the one just described. The only difference was that it rested on a framework attached to a single wheel directly underneath. This cross between a wheelbarrow and a sedan-chair was supported and trundled along the street by four bearers.

On this journey, however, Yung Pak and his companions were to ride on ponies.

The Korean ponies are small, fine-coated animals, little larger than Shetland ponies. They are very tough and strong, and can endure long marches with little food. They are sometimes obstinate and are desperate fighters, squealing and neighing on all occasions. They often attack other ponies, and never become friendly with each other on a journey. In their attacks upon one another loads are forgotten and often seriously damaged. Notwithstanding, they bear with much patience a great deal of abuse from unkind masters. Because of much beating and overloading, they are generally a sorry-looking lot of animals.

Ki Pak had to engage ponies for himself, Yung Pak, and Wang Ken. He was also obliged to employ a cook for the journey, who had to have a pony to carry along the kettles and pans and other utensils. It was also necessary to hire body-servants and several ponies to carry luggage, and as each pony must have a mapu, or groom, it made quite a procession when the party started out of Seoul on the journey to the northeast.

It was a fine day when the start was made. It was not early in the morning, for, if there is anything a Korean hates to do, it is to make an early start on a journey. If you had been in Yung Pak's place, you would have gone crazy with impatience. The servants were late in bringing around the ponies, and the process of loading them was a very slow one.

But Yung Pak had long before learned to be patient under such circumstances. In fact, he seemed to care little whether the start were made in the morning or at noon. He calmly watched the servants at their work, and, when at last all was declared ready, he gravely mounted his pony and fell into the procession behind his father, with Wang Ken immediately following.

A most comical sight was the cook, perched on top of his load of pans, pots, and potatoes. As his pony trotted along with the others, it looked as if the cook was in constant danger of a fall from his lofty seat, but he sat as calm and unconcerned as one could imagine.

You would laugh if you should see the strings of eggs hanging across this pony's back—yes, eggs. They were packed in bands of wheat straw, and between each pair of eggs a straw was twisted. Thus a straw rope enclosing twenty or more eggs, well protected, was made and thrown over the top of the load.

Other riders had more comfortable seats, for most of the ponies carried baggage in two wicker baskets,—one strapped upon each side,—and on top of these was piled bedding and wadded clothing, which made a soft seat for the rider.

The mapus who accompanied the procession were dressed in short cotton jackets, loose trousers, with sandals and cotton wrappings upon the feet. They had to step lively to keep up with the ponies.

All the people in this company carried with them long garments made of oiled paper. You have already learned that the Korean paper is very tough, and when soaked with oil it forms a splendid protection against the rain. Many of these garments had a very peculiar appearance, because they were made of paper on which had been set copies for schoolboys to use in learning to write.

As Yung Pak and his companions passed along the dirty streets of Seoul toward a gate in the great wall, a curious crowd was attracted by the unusual sight. This mob of men and boys were good-natured, but very curious, and it gathered so close as to impede the progress of the ponies. Moreover, a watchful eye had to be kept on all the luggage, lest some over-covetous person might steal the provisions and supplies on the ponies' backs.

Notwithstanding the slow progress made by Ki Pak's company, it took only a short time to pass through the narrow streets and out by the great gate, leaving behind the noisy mob of men and boys who had followed them to the city's wall.

Once outside, upon the road which wound around and over the high hills that surround the city, the pure country air seemed very sweet and refreshing to Yung Pak, who knew nothing of life outside Seoul. This was his first journey into the country, and the many strange sights drew exclamations of surprise and wonder from him. The green waving grass and swaying foliage of the trees were ever new sources of joy and pleasure, and the delicate odours which the breezes bore to his sensitive nostrils were refreshing and life-giving.

Among the strange sights which attracted Yung Pak's attention, as they rode along through the country, were some very curious figures erected by the roadside. These were posts, one side of which was roughly planed. On the upper part of each of these posts was a rude carving of a hideous human face with prominent teeth. The cheeks and teeth were slightly coloured. A most fiendish appearance was presented by these figures, called by the Koreans syou-sal-mak-i, and if looks counted for anything, they ought well to serve their purpose,—the scaring away of evil spirits from the village near which the figures always stood. The mile-posts, or fjang-seung, along the way were often similarly decorated.

ON THE UPPER PART OF EACH OF THESE POSTS WAS A RUDE CARVING

Another curiosity by the wayside which led to wonder on Yung Pak's part was an old trunk of a tall tree. For about thirty feet from the ground this was painted in coloured stripes very much like a barber's pole. The top and branches of the tree had been trimmed off, and the upper end was rudely carved in a shape representing a dragon with a forked tail. From the head, which resembled that of an alligator, hung various cords, to which were attached small brass bells and a wooden fish. Wang Ken told Yung Pak that this was a monument to some famous Korean "doctor of literature."

On the first day's journey toward Chang-an-sa the party made good progress. The plan was to get to Yong-pyöng, about twenty miles from Seoul, before nightfall. To you this would seem a short day's journey, but when it is remembered that many of the servants were on foot, and that the little ponies were heavily loaded, it does not seem so strange that more ground could not be covered in one day. In addition, in many places the roads were poor, though in the valleys there was a smooth bottom where the sand had washed down from the hills.

On some of these hillsides little villages were perched. Yung Pak noticed that on the upper side of each of these hill-towns was a moon-shaped wall.

"What is that wall for?" he asked Wang Ken as they passed one.

"That protects the village in time of rainstorms," replied the tutor. "The soil here is of such a nature that it easily washes away, and if the town were unprotected the earth would soon be swept from beneath the houses. If you will look sharply, you will see outside the wall a deep trench which carries off the rushing water."

As they were slowly riding along a road which wound around and over a high hill Yung Pak still kept his eyes wide open for strange sights. Suddenly he lifted his arm, and, pointing toward a tree upon a little hill at one side of the road, he said to Wang Ken:

"Oh, what a queer-looking tree that is! And are not those strange leaves on it? What kind of a tree is it, anyway?"

"Ha, ha!" laughed Wang Ken, "I don't wonder that you call that a strange-looking tree. Let's take a walk up to it and get a closer view."

So the ponies were halted, and down sprang Yung Pak and Wang Ken. Leaving the ponies in charge of the mapus, they marched up the hill to get a nearer sight of the tree.

"Why," said the boy, as they approached it, "those are not leaves that we saw from the road, but they are rags and strips of cloth. It looks as if some one had hung out their clothes to dry and forgotten to take them in again. What does it all mean?"

"That tree, my boy," Wang Ken replied, "is called the sacred devil-tree. That is a queer combination of names, but you know there are a lot of ignorant people in our country who are very superstitious. They believe in all sorts of evil and good spirits. They think these spirits watch every act of their lives. Consequently they do all they can to please the good spirits and to drive away the evil ones. This tree they believe has power to keep off the bad spirits, so every man who thinks that a demon has possession of him tears a piece of cloth from his garment and carefully ties it to a branch. That is how all these strips you see come to be hanging above you. Some have hung there so long that the wind and rain have torn them to rags."

"Yes, but why is this done?" asked Yung Pak.

"Because," was the reply, "a man who is possessed by an evil spirit thinks that by thus tying a part of his clothing to the tree he may induce the spirit to attach himself to it instead of to his own person."

Yung Pak's curiosity satisfied, they returned to the road, mounted their ponies, and quickly caught up with the rest of the party.

No further incidents of special importance marked this first day's journey, and shortly before nightfall they arrived at the town of Yong-pyŏng. They found the village inn to be a series of low, small buildings built on three sides of a courtyard. Into low sheds in this yard the ponies were crowded and the luggage removed from their backs. Ki Pak's servants proceeded to build a fire in the centre of the yard and the cook made preparations for getting supper. Travellers had to provide a large part of their own meals, for, as already stated, these village inns were not hotels in the real sense of the word. They were simply rude lodging-places where travellers might be protected from the night air and have a chance to sleep while passing through the country.

Into the main waiting-room of the inn Yung Pak, with his father and tutor, entered. At the door they removed their shoes and left them outside. In the room were several other travellers seated upon the floor, which was covered with oiled paper and grass mats. There was absolutely no furniture. The walls were covered with clean white paper. Each man in the room was smoking a pipe, which consisted of a brass bowl and a reed stem over three feet long. All wore long white robes, though one of the occupants had hung his hat upon the wall.

Into this room after a time the cook brought supper for his masters. Other servants brought in boxes which were used as tables, and though the style was not just what Yung Pak was used to, he managed to eat a hearty meal. The day in the open air had given him a hunger and a zest he rarely knew.

After supper, for a short time Yung Pak and Wang Ken talked over with Ki Pak the events of the day. A servant soon announced that their sleeping-rooms were ready, and they gladly at once sought their beds. To get to their rooms they again stepped out into the courtyard. They found that each bedroom was one of the little buildings facing the yard. Yung Pak and Wang Ken occupied one room, while Ki Pak had a room by himself. Through a narrow door about three feet high the lad and his tutor entered their room. The door was simply a lattice shutter covered with paper. The room was very small,—barely space for the two mattresses which had been put there by the servants, and the ceiling was so low that even the short

Koreans could hardly stand upright. Yet here our two friends managed to make themselves very comfortable for the night.

Outside in the courtyard the fire was kept burning, beside which two watchmen sat all night smoking and telling stories. It was necessary to maintain a watch till morning because the country districts of Korea are infested with wild animals, particularly tigers, and the bright blaze of the fire served to keep them at a distance. Otherwise the thin-walled houses would have been slight protection for the sleeping travellers.

As it was, Yung Pak slept soundly the whole night, and did not awake until after daylight, when servants brought to his door a wooden bowl and a brass vessel full of water for his morning bath. Quickly he sprang up, and with his companions made ready for the day's journey, for they were all anxious to be on their way.

THE DAY WAS PASSED IN MUCH THE SAME MANNER AS THE PRECEDING ONE

Breakfast was served in much the same manner as the supper of the previous evening had been. Of this meal all heartily partook, for a Korean is never guilty of having a poor appetite.

As usual, it took a long time to get the ponies properly loaded and ready to start, and the forenoon was about half-gone when the procession finally left the courtyard of the inn.

A twenty-mile march would bring the party to Rang-chyön, where it was proposed to spend the second night of the journey.

The day was passed in much the same manner as the preceding one, though of course new scenes proved ever interesting to Yung Pak. During this day the party had to cross a river which was too deep to ford, and over which there was no sort of bridge. For the assistance of travellers a ferry-boat had been provided. This boat was a broad, flat-bottomed, clumsy affair. It could carry but three ponies at a time, with several men. The men in charge of the boat were slow and obstinate, and consequently it took a long time for all to get across the river.

It was right here that an unfortunate, yet laughable, accident occurred.

As on the preceding day, the cook rode perched upon his pony's load of kettles, pans, and pots. When riding along a good road his position was precarious enough, requiring all his best efforts to maintain his balance.

When his turn came to go upon the ferry-boat, Ki Pak advised him to dismount and lead his pony across the plank which covered the watery space between the bank of the river and the boat. But the cook was an obstinate Korean, as well as a trifle lazy, and refused to get down, thinking he could safely drive his beast across the gang-plank. Ordinarily this would have been possible, but on this particular occasion, just as the pony stepped upon the plank, the boat gave a lurch, the plank slipped, and overboard went pony, cook, and all. For a few moments there was enough bustle and excitement to suit any one. Fortunately, the water was not deep, and quickly the drenched animal and man were pulled from the water. The only permanent harm was to some of the provisions that were a part of the pony's load. The cook was a wiser as well as a wet man, and made up his mind that the next time he would heed the advice to dismount when boarding a ferry-boat.

The day's journey was completed without further special incident, and at night they rested in the inn at Rang-chyön under conditions much the same as at Yong-pyöng.

The third day's journey brought the company to Kewen-syong. On the way thither Yung Pak was much interested in the sights of the country, which grew wilder and more strange the farther they got from Seoul. On this day numerous highwaymen were met, but they dared not molest the travellers on account of the large number in the party.

The cabins along the country roads were a continual source of curiosity to Yung Pak. They were built of mud, without windows, and no door except a screen of cords. In nearly every doorway would be sitting a man, smoking a long-stemmed pipe, who looked with wide-open eyes at the unusual procession passing his house.

Of course all the men who lived in these country cabins were farmers, and Yung Pak liked to watch them as they worked in their fields, for to the city-bred boy this is always an entrancing sight. What seemed most curious to him was the fact that women were also at work in the fields. At his home the women of the family nearly always stayed in their own apartments, and when they did go out always went heavily veiled. These country women not only assisted in the farm work, but they had to do all the spinning and weaving for the family, in addition to usual household cares.

Wang Ken was able to tell Yung Pak much about country life, for, like most of the school-masters of Korea, he was himself a farmer's son. He told how the Korean farmer lived a simple, patient life, while at the same time he was ignorant and superstitious. He believed in demons, spirits, and dragons, and in nearly every house were idols in honour of the imaginary deities.

Pigs and bulls are the chief animals on Korean farms. The latter are used as beasts of burden, though occasionally a more prosperous man may own a pony or a donkey. The farming tools are extremely rude and simple, thus necessitating the labour of several men or women where one man could do the work with good tools.

While travelling along Yung Pak met several hunters. They were not an uncommon sight on the streets of Seoul. When in the city they wore a rough felt conical hat and dark blue cotton robe. The garments were ugly in appearance and inconvenient. When the hunters were after game the robe was discarded, and its place taken by a short wadded jacket, its sleeves bound around the arms over wadded cuffs which reached from wrist to elbow. In a similar way the trousers were bound to the calf of the hunter's leg, and light straw sandals over a long piece of cotton cloth were strapped to the feet and ankles. A huge string game-bag was slung over his back, and in an antelope's horn or a crane's bill bullets were carried. Powder was kept dry in a tortoise-shaped case of leather or oiled paper.

Yung Pak's father would have been glad to have taken time for seeking game with some of these hunters, but the business of his trip prevented any unnecessary delay on the journey.

CHAPTER VIII.

THE MONASTERY AT CHANG-AN-SA

In the latter part of the afternoon of the fourth day, our travellers, weary and worn with the long journey, came in sight of Chang-an-sa, the Temple of Eternal Rest, one of the oldest monasteries of Korea, where hundreds of monks devoted their lives to the service of Buddha.

The temple buildings, with deep curved roofs, are in a glorious situation on a small level lot of grassy land crowded between the high walls of a rocky ravine.

Yung Pak was delighted at his first sight of the great temple and the surrounding buildings. Through the swaying branches of the forest-trees he caught brief glimpses of the granite walls and turrets reddening in the sunset glow. The deepening gloom of the gorge was lighted by the slant beams of the setting sun, and on the water in the stream below flecks of foam sparkled and danced in the light of the dying day.

At first conversation was out of the question in the presence of such a majestic display of nature's wonders combined with the handiwork of man.

Coming to a gate of red stone, Yung Pak asked the meaning of the carved arrow in the arch overhead.

"That arrow," replied his father, "signifies that the temples to which this gate is the outer entrance are under the patronage of the king. Wherever you see that sign, you may know that the king has a special interest, and his messengers will be treated with respect and hospitality. Consequently we may expect to be well cared for during our visit to this place."

Passing through the gate, our friends found themselves at once in the midst of the Chang-an-sa monastery buildings. In addition to the great chief temple, there were many smaller places of worship, with bell and tablet houses. There were also cells and sleeping-rooms for the monks, servants' quarters, stables, a huge kitchen, and an immense dining-room, together with a large guest-hall and a nunnery. In addition there were several buildings devoted to the care of the aged, the infirm, and the sick. All these places, during his stay, Yung Pak visited in company with Wang Ken and guided by one of the monks.

Besides the buildings already mentioned there were several houses that had been erected by the king on purpose for the use of his officials, and it was to one of these that Ki Pak and his son and Wang Ken were led by several of the priests of the monastery. In the meantime, the servants and the ponies were cared for in other places assigned for the purpose.

Yung Pak was not sorry to arrive at his journey's end, even though he had enjoyed himself every moment of the time since he left Seoul. A four days' ride on the back of a pony will make the most enthusiastic traveller tired, and Yung Pak was glad to get to bed in the comfortable room provided just as soon as he had eaten his supper. His night's sleep was a sound one, though at midnight, and again at four o'clock in the morning, he was awakened by the ringing of bells and gongs that called the monks to the worship of Buddha.

In the morning Yung Pak awoke greatly refreshed, and, after a bountiful breakfast, he started out with Wang Ken, guided by a monk, to see the wonders of Chang-an-sa monastery.

One of the first things he noticed was the large number of boys about the place. He learned from the guide that these lads were all orphans who were being cared for by the priests, and who, later in life, would themselves become priests of Buddha. They were all bright and active, and were kept busily employed as waiters and errand-runners when they were not at work on their studies. Like most boys, however, they managed to get a generous share of time for play.

It would be impossible to tell in detail about all the strange things Yung Pak saw at this monastery. The chief temple was an enormous structure of stone and tile and carved wood, all decorated in gorgeous combinations of red, green, gold, and white.

Within this temple was one room called the "chamber of imagery." Inside its darkened walls a single monk chanted his monotonous prayer before an altar. During the chant he also occupied himself by striking a small bell with a deer-horn. Bells played a great part in the worship at Chang-an-sa, and all the prayers were emphasized by the clanging of bells great or small.

Along the shadowy walls of this room could be seen the weapons, as well as the eyes and teeth, the legs and arms, of gods and demons otherwise invisible. These had a ghostly effect on Yung Pak, and made him cling closely to the side of his tutor.

Above the altar before which the priest knelt was an immense carving in imitation of an uprooted tree. Among the roots thus exposed were placed fifty-three idols in all kinds of positions. Beneath the carving were represented three fierce-looking dragons, on whose faces were signs of the most awful torment and suffering.

"About this altar-piece," said Yung Pak's guide, "there is a legend you might like to hear."

"Oh, yes," was the reply, "tell us the story."

"Many years ago," began the guide, "fifty-three Buddhist priests came from India to Korea for the purpose of converting the people to their belief. When they reached this place they were very tired, and sat down by a spring beneath the wide-spreading branches of a tree. They had not been there long when three dragons appeared and attacked the priests. During the contest the dragons called up a great wind which uprooted the tree. In return, each of the priests placed an image of Buddha on a tree-root, turning it into an altar. Thus they were able to overcome the dragons, who were forced into the spring. On top of them great stones were piled, and afterward the monastery of Chang-an-sa was built upon the site of the battle between the priests and the dragons."

Afterward Yung Pak visited the great kitchens, the dining-rooms, the stables, the private rooms of the monks, and every place which might be of interest to an inquisitive boy of his age.

During the time he remained at Chang-an-sa he made several excursions into the surrounding country, but always returning to the monastery at night.

Meanwhile Ki Pak had transacted the business for which he came to this region, and at the end of ten days was ready to return to Seoul.

Of this journey it is not necessary to tell. No mishap marred the pleasure of the trip, and all returned safe and sound to their home in the capital city of Korea. Yung Pak had enjoyed the journey very, very much, yet he was not sorry once more to be among the familiar scenes and surroundings of home.

CHAPTER IX.

A FULL-FLEDGED TOP-KNOT

Like all Korean boys, Yung Pak wore his hair in two braids, and by the time he was twelve years old these had become very long, and hung in black and glossy plaits down his back.

On the day that he was thirteen his father called him to his room and told the lad that the time had come for him to assume the dignities of a man. In accordance with that statement, he had decided that on the next day his son should be formally "invested" with the top-knot. In other words, the crown of his head was to be shaven, and his long hair tightly coiled upon the bare place thus made. This is called the "Investiture of the Top-knot," and is always attended by solemn ceremonies.

In preparation for this event Ki Pak had made careful and elaborate arrangements. He had provided for his son new clothes and a hat after the style of his own. He had also consulted an eminent astrologer, who had chosen the propitious day and hour for the ceremony after due consultation of the calendar and the stars and planets in their courses.

Generally, if the father is blessed with good fortune and a number of sons, he acts as his own master of ceremonies on such an occasion, but as Ki Pak had only this one son he decided to ask his brother, Wu-pom Nai, who had several sons and was a prosperous merchant of Seoul, to fill this important position.

Yung Pak could hardly wait for the morrow to come. So excited was he at the thought of the great honour that was to be his that he spent almost a sleepless night. However, like all nights, long or short, this one passed, and the wished-for hour at last arrived.

All the male members of the family were present. Korean women are reckoned of little importance and take no part in social and family affairs. On this occasion no men except relatives were asked to attend.

Yung Pak was directed to seat himself on the floor in the centre of the room, facing the east. This was the point of compass revealed by the astrologer as most favourable to the young candidate for manly honours.

With great deliberation and much formality Wu-pom Nai proceeded to loosen the boy's heavy plaits of hair.

Then with great care, while the onlookers watched with breathless interest, he shaved the crown of the lad's head, making a bare circular spot about three inches in diameter. Over this spot he twisted all the remaining hair into a coil about four inches long, pointing slightly forward like a horn.

Over the top-knot thus made the master of ceremonies placed the mang-kun, which was a crownless skull-cap made of a very delicate stiff gauze. This was tied on very tightly,—so tightly that it made a deep ridge in Yung Pak's forehead and gave him a severe headache; but he bore the pain heroically and without flinching—for was he not now a man? The regular Korean man's hat, with its flapping wings, was next put on, and this part of the ceremony was complete.

Yung Pak now rose from his position, and made a deep bow to each one in the room, beginning with his father, and then in regular order according to relationship. Afterward, accompanied by his relatives, he proceeded to the room where were placed the tablets in memory of his ancestors. There he offered sacrifice before each one in turn.

Lighted candles in brass candlesticks he placed in front of each tablet, and beside the candles he put dishes of sacrificial food and fruit. Then, as before his living relatives,

he bowed profoundly to the tablets of the dead ones, and formally and seriously let them know that he had been regularly invested with the top-knot, and now had the right to be regarded as a man.

The sacrifices made, Yung Pak called at the homes of all the male friends of the family, who now for the first time looked upon him as their equal, and in the evening Ki Pak gave a great dinner in honour of his son. Here there was much feasting and rejoicing, and all united in wishing the greatest prosperity and lifelong happiness to the little Korean boy now become a man.

He is no longer our little Korean cousin. Hence, we leave him at this point, joining heartily in the best wishes and the compliments bestowed upon him by his friends. 45

THE END.